THE DREAM QUILT

THE
DREAM
QUILT

Amy Zerner
&
Jessie Spicer Zerner

Charles E. Tuttle Company, Inc.
Boston • Rutland, Vermont • Tokyo

Published in 1995 by
CHARLES E. TUTTLE COMPANY, INC.
of Rutland, Vermont and Tokyo, Japan
with editorial offices at 153 Milk Street, 5th floor,
Boston, Massachusetts 02109

Library of Congress Cataloging-in-Publication Data

Zerner, Amy.
  The dream quilt/Amy Zerner & Jessie Spicer Zerner.
    p. cm.
  Summary: After touching the patches of a magic quilt, Alex has a series of adventurous dreams.
  ISBN 0-8048-1999-8

  [1. Dreams—Fiction. 2. Magic—Fiction.] I. Spicer-Zerner,
Jessie, ill. II. Title.
PZ7.Z445Dr 1994   94-36011
[Fic]—dc20   CIP
                                       AC

First Edition
1 3 5 7 9 10 8 6 4 2

Text Design by Kathryn Sky-Peck and Fran Skelly
Jacket Design by Sherry Fatla

Printed in China

Contents

The First Night

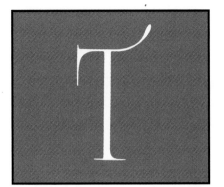here's the sea!" shouted Alex as he looked out of the tiny attic window.

He had come to spend a week at his Aunt Rachel's house, his very first vacation away from home.

He had never been on a ship or even on a train before his trip here. It had felt as if he were riding inside a great animal puffing along, filling the air with smoke and sparks. His father and mother had waved from the station platform until they had seemed to disappear. The familiar city buildings had grown small, and open land had appeared with farms, cows, and horses. Once in a while, a windmill could be seen. He felt as if he were going back in time from a busy, modern city to the past where his grandfather, Aunt Rachel's brother, had been a boy very like himself.

"It will be exciting," his mother had told him. "There's nothing like that first trip on your own. It's part of growing up."

Then there it was—Sea Horse Cove! The conductor came to get him and delivered him to Aunt Rachel. She had crinkles around her brown eyes and a smile almost ready to come out but held back while she seemed to be deciding what sort of a boy he was. Holding out her hand, she shook his firmly.

Once at her house, Aunt Rachel showed him to the attic room where he would be sleeping. The first thing he wanted to see was the view from his window. "Well," she said, "finally!" Then she grinned widely like a kid. Alex felt happy and relieved as if he had just passed a test.

He stared at all the water stretching out under the sky and the grey waves getting bigger and bigger until their tops, trimmed in lace, curled over and smashed down upon the beach. Far off were faint silhouettes of boats or ships, he was never quite sure which was which.

"Your great-great-grandfather was the captain of a ship," said Aunt Rachel's voice behind him, startling him back to the present. "That's his chest by the bottom of the bed. He used to balance it on his shoulder and off to sea he'd go."

Alex looked about the small room. There was a banged-up old bureau, a rag rug, and a salty, old, dark leather chest with straps and brass studs at the foot of the white, metal bed.

"Was he a pirate?" Alex asked.

Aunt Rachel laughed and said you could probably find a pirate or two in any respectable family.

"Let's go get some apples for a pie," she suggested. "You could climb right out that window and meet me outside. That old tree has

been standing there since I was your age. Its apples made my first pie and will probably make my last."

"I'll go with you," said Alex, never having climbed a tree. He sometimes sat out on the fire escape of his apartment building when it was hot, but that wasn't

really climbing, and he was a little afraid to try a tree. There weren't many on the city street where he lived. Those were dusty and dirty and greatly admired by dogs. Mothers discouraged their children from climbing them, by reminding them darkly that they "might fall and hurt themselves."

In no time at all, they had picked a basketful of apples. "Why don't you run down to the beach while I start dinner," Aunt Rachael said as she went into the kitchen.

There was a brisk breeze blowing as Alex went down the hill to the water. Big rocks ran out to meet the waves, and there were piles of seaweed, which he kicked with his foot. Funny little shells ran out balanced on dainty crab's legs. There were peach-colored shells like ladies' fans and a big, brown thing that looked like a helmet with a spike on one end. Alex jumped back nervously as it moved slowly into the water and disappeared.

"I wonder how many of *those* are underneath the ocean?" he thought. "Or how many other weird things? Like those enormous fish with teeth from dinosaur days."

Half of an orange sun floated above the ocean. The bubbling, foamy waves came closer and grabbed at his sneakers. His stomach gave a sudden lurch. He did have a big imagination, people said. Sometimes it raced ahead of his everyday thoughts and led him into stories that he knew weren't real, but that could make his heart beat faster.

At that moment, he heard his Aunt's voice calling him so he hurried towards the grey-shingled house where the lights were already shining dimly in the windows.

"Ready to eat?" his Aunt smiled. "Macaroni and cheese, and salad from the garden."

"I grew those vegetables," she said, observing his downturned mouth. "They're just picked and good for you. Also," she added primly, "no salad, no pie."

Alex saw the pie and smelled it too. The goodness of it made his mouth water.

Plates were licked clean, salad and all.

"It's remarkable the appetite a little salt air gives you," said his Aunt with a sigh. "Let's leave the dishes in the sink; I'll get them later."

They went to sit in front of the old fireplace in the living room. A fire was burning, ready for Alex, and pinecones snapped and sparkled in the flames.

"It's getting a little nippy these evenings," remarked Aunt Rachel. "Too cold to go swimming, but we can take a picnic to the beach. Toast franks and marshmallows, too. Sound good?"

"Uh-huh," answered Alex, too full to think of more food. He felt as wide awake as an owl.

"How about a game?" inquired his Aunt, wisely realizing Alex wasn't ready for bed.

They played "Battleship" and "Hang Man" for what seemed

like hours, and Alex won quite a few times, much to his Aunt's surprise.

She finally threw her pencil down. "Well, that does it," she yawned. "You're beating me too often; You'll have to pay a penalty.

"I've got to go to bed," she said, laughing at his alarmed face. "So do you." She tugged him by the hand up the creaky, narrow stairs to the attic.

"I'll leave the light on in the hall so you can see your way about."

"What if I can't sleep?" asked Alex.

His Aunt Rachel looked at him solemnly for a moment, "I'll tell you what, there's something in that pirate chest that'll cure that. Open it up and see what you find."

As he raised the lid, there was a strong smell of moth balls. "This?" he pulled out an old quilt made of many patches and looked at it in disappointment.

"Yes, *this*," his Aunt answered, her eyes sparkling. "Your great-great-grandmother made it for your great-greatgrandfather, and it has been all around the world.

"Who knows what sights it has seen," she mused.

Alex stared at the quilt curiously and saw the colors begin to glow. There were blues and greens ("like the ocean," Aunt Rachel said), and pinks, oranges, and golds that shimmered and moved,

appearing as strange flowers or odd, unknown animals. Some
patches were of old lace, beads, or ribbons in patterns of
stars and diamonds. There were stitched hearts of red
and purple, and little pictures from long ago.

As he got into bed, the cold sheets felt frosty. Aunt
Rachel shook out the quilt and tucked it in around
him.

"What if I can't sleep?" he asked again, anx-
iously, but already he could feel the quilt warming
his toes with a fine glowing heat.

"Oh," he heard his Aunt's quiet voice whisper. "You'll
have a wonderful sleep tonight. It's a dream quilt, you
know."

The light from the hallway fell through the half-opened door
and seemed to shine most brightly on one particular patch. It had a
design of silken red and yellow maple leaves and, as his fingers slid
over its smooth surfaces, his eyes shut.

☽

I t seemed but a moment before his eyes opened again. It
was daytime, and he was half-squinting in the light of
the setting sun. To his surprise, he had a rake over his
shoulder. In front of him a long row of leaf piles
stretched across a small clearing bounded by trees. He felt very warm
and rather tired—as if he had been working hard.

Wiping the wetness off his forehead, he noticed a sudden stirring in the largest pile of leaves, as if a strong wind blew, but the air was still. A row of large, leaf-like shapes appeared while the setting sun hit them with a red metallic glow. At the same moment, a thin thread of smoke arose.

"A fire!" thought Alex, running forward and reaching out with his rake to beat down the flames. The whole leaf pile shivered and swirled, and a rather small dragon stepped out. His eyes were the shiny brown of chestnuts and, as he opened his mouth, another, fainter, twist of smoke emerged with a strong smell, like wet ashes after a fire. For some reason, perhaps because the whole scene was so dream-like, Alex felt no fear.

"What are you doing here?" Alex asked rather brusquely.

The dragon looked puzzled. "I'm not quite sure," he mumbled, casting his eyes about as if looking for an answer. "I went to sleep some time ago . . ." he trailed off looking upwards at a small cloud in the sky. "And then," he paused as his eyes followed the downward fall of a leaf with brief interest, "I awoke here." He gestured vaguely at the ground. "It must have been," he added, staring in surprise at Alex as if seeing him for the first time, "several hundred years ago." He yawned widely, displaying an alarming row of sharp, green teeth.

"He certainly doesn't brush," thought Alex disapprovingly. And then he added aloud and rather unkindly, "There aren't dragons anymore, you know."

The dragon's eyes widened in shock and disbelief. "No dragons?" he sidled closer to Alex who noticed that the dragon had scales like a fish in beautiful tints of red, blue, and violet.

"Who fights the knights then?" the dragon demanded. "Who eats the damsels?"

Alex wasn't quite sure what a "damsel" was, but as the dragon came closer he felt a little uneasy. "That was ever so long ago," he said in a loud, brave voice. "Now," he added, "dragons are absolutely useless. They're only in picture books, and I don't even like those stories."

The dragon shut his eyes suddenly and placed a paw upon his forehead. One long teardrop slid down his cheek and sparkled briefly. "May I just go home with you then?" he asked in a choked voice. "I will try to be helpful."

Alex did not respond but let the dragon follow as he walked slowly towards a house just visible in the distance. It seemed to be his Aunt Rachel's house and Alex suddenly remembered that he was a visitor there and that he had had apple pie last night, but everything else seemed a little different. The ocean was not to be seen at all, for instance, and in its place was a forest of trees in fall colors.

The next moment he heard the dragon's voice in his ear. "I can toast marshmallows," it said, "and melt a path in the snow and get the kettle to boil very quickly . . ."

Alex laughed. In a few minutes they were sitting, drinking apple-cinnamon tea, in front of a roaring fire that the dragon had lit in his Aunt's fireplace. They sat facing each other in great soft chairs that smelled faintly of camphor. From a leather pouch that hung at his side, the dragon produced a small clay pipe and smoked white clouds which wreathed his head. The smoke and the heat made Alex very sleepy.

"What else can you do?" he asked drowsily.

The dragon's voice seemed to come from far away. "I am a great storyteller," he said, "With more stories to tell than patches on a quilt. And," he added, "I'm sure we'll meet again." He rubbed his brow sleepily with one paw. "Dragons tell dream tales. You'll enjoy that. It is the most magical way of story-telling. You are *in* the story, not just listening. And I," he added, leaning forward intently and fixing Alex with his wide eyes, "will be there too. I was once an actor and I still love to perform. I still love a change of costume—a disguise. We'll play a game," he chuckled merrily, "our own little game called, 'Find the dragon!'"

"Dragons," he went on, without a trace of modesty, "are very wise. Their long-ago wisdom still has its uses in

11

the present and the future. We have kept this old world steady in
many a storm."

"Can you see the future?" murmured Alex.

"Well, I can see that we'll meet again and that we'll always be
great friends."

A log fell in a shower of bright sparks, and the heat seemed to
touch Alex's face as he awoke to the sun shining brightly through the
open window. He smelled burning leaves and, when he looked out,
saw his Aunt below tending a bonfire.

"Any dragons down there?" he shouted, leaning from the window.

"Not a one," his Aunt Rachel called back, laughing. "Come
down to breakfast. You sure had a good night's sleep!"

Before he left the attic room, Alex folded the quilt up carefully. Doing so, he noticed the patch with the silken maple leaves, a forest in the background, and, looking more closely among the trees, he
saw a glimpse of something red, blue, and violet. His heart skipped
with excitement as he wondered what he would dream of next.

The Second Night

hen Alex awoke he could hear the sound of waves and seagulls calling over the water. A wonderful smell tickled his nose and seemed to pull him out of bed and down the stairs to the kitchen. Pancakes!

"Take plenty of maple syrup," his Aunt told him, "and use that orange juice to wash it all down."

"Where are *your* pancakes?" asked Alex after he had finished the very last one.

"In my stomach. Just where yours are. I let you sleep late this morning, but I ate early. Now you skedaddle and take a look around the place."

As Alex went down the back steps, he saw the apple tree shining in the sun. He bravely imagined himself sitting on its very top branch. From up there he would have been able to see his great-great-grandfather's ship returning from long-ago adventures. Of course the apple tree had only been an apple seed back then. The sea was still there, though, as it had been then. It sparkled at the bottom of the hill and stretched out towards the horizon.

Alex hurried down to walk along the beach. The water seeped through his sneakers and was squishy and cold between his toes. Little wet stones sparkled like precious jewels, but when he picked the prettiest ones and spread them on the sand, they dried and turned dull and ordinary. He walked slowly back up the hill feeling his cold toes turning hot and itchy. Aunt Rachel laughed when she saw his feet.

"Aren't boys the oddest things?" she said, "they just can't get near water without getting wet. Except when it's in a bathtub," she added, "with some soap."

After his bath Alex learned what "chores" were. Things like going to the post box when the mail truck chugged up the road to the house, dusting every last cobweb off the porch's screened windows, shucking corn for supper, and drying the dishes that stood in a metal rack.

Aunt Rachel had just gotten around to washing them.

"Of course, they'll dry themselves if you wait long enough," said Aunt Rachel reasonably, "but we'll need those dishes for supper and the blueberry cobbler."

After dinner they grinned at each other to see who had the bluest teeth.

The orange sun seemed to fall into the sea while they rocked on the porch chairs. The stars popped out as the sky turned black. Millions of them hung in the sky. The city with all its lights was no match for their brightness. The stars' shimmer tickled his eyes and made him sleepy. The crickets sang their lullabies, and suddenly the thought of seeing the dragon again made Alex feel like snuggling under his great-great-grandfather's quilt.

As before, one patch seemed to outshine the others in the hall light that fell through the open door. It was of a ribbed material, grey and dark blue, with a pattern of green pine needles at its top and tiny brown pinecones strewn along its bottom. Alex stroked the rough surface. It felt like the bark of a tree.

After a short time, Alex was not at all surprised to find himself in a forest of evergreens. The light was dim, and it was very quiet. The fallen needles were like a soft, slippery carpet. When he looked up, he could barely see the sky except for one or two early stars. Moving cautiously forward, he suddenly saw some sparkles of red.

"Aha," he thought with a gasp of excitement, "the dragon!"

He slipped and slid recklessly towards his goal until he emerged abruptly into a small glade lit by a fire with the flames he had seen. In front of a campfire sat a very small, grey, hooded figure who looked up as Alex appeared through the trees.

"Oh," said Alex disappointedly, "I thought you were a dragon."

There was a faint, whispery chuckle, and Alex was shocked to see a number of shiny black eyes as the creature turned its head. Could there be eight?

"Surely not," thought Alex in hor-

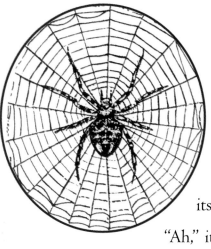

ror. "Is it some sort of very small but very awful monster?"

The grey figure looked at Alex too, although with so many eyes it was hard to tell exactly where its glance fell.

"Ah," its shadowy voice rose questioningly. "You are a—boy?" The last word came out in hesitation, as if it had never been used before in conversation.

"Yes," said Alex firmly. He did not add, "And what are you?" It did not seem quite polite.

"Sit down by the fire," the grey figure offered. "It's too dark to travel further this night."

Alex sat down and hugged his knees. The fire was lovely and warm. He found two apples in his pocket and offered one to his host or . . . hostess?

"No thanks," was the reply, "but perhaps you'd want some of this?" The creature held a small bundle of silvery material through which Alex could just see part of a wing and some thin, leg-like things.

Alex jammed the apple quickly into his mouth. "I've got plenty to eat," he mumbled. "I'm really not very hungry."

He cautiously examined his neighbor, observing its grey cloak and hood, noting that several grey arms and a number of legs appeared and disappeared beneath its folds as the creature opened and ate the contents of its little packets. The warm fire and the quiet made Alex relax. After all, he was a good deal bigger than his companion, who seemed unlikely to pick a fight.

"What are you called?" Alex inquired, hoping to find out more.

"My name is Maude," came the soft answer. "I am an arachnid."

"An arachnid?"

"A spider. I'm on my way to the tower to deliver the princess's lace wedding veil. It's a beautiful thing," she said proudly. She pulled a dark, velvet pouch from beneath her cloak and opened it to show Alex a gleam of fine silver threads intricately knotted. "It must be there by tomorrow. Oh, how beautiful she will be," sighed Maude. "And how sad the occasion."

"Sad?" queried Alex, who had immediately imagined a grand party with all sorts of wonderful food and iced cakes in all shapes and sizes.

"She's marrying Tarantella," said Maude grimly. "He's a horrible stag beetle and she's just a girl not much bigger than you. He'll soon have his great claws on her. Now they have her shut away in a tower room and she'll never escape."

The flames sputtered and Maude added some pinecones and branches to the fire. There was a short silence, and then she asked, "Would you like an adventure? You look like a lad who might like some excitement."

"Yes," said Alex with a quick intake of breath. After all, he had come expecting to find a dragon. "What sort of an adventure?"

Maude looked at him briefly. "A good sort. I need a little help, you see, and you're just the one that's wanted."

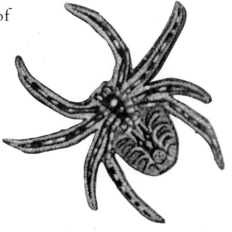

"Oh," said Alex, feeling rather brave and proud. "Alright. When will it happen?"

"Very soon now!" said Maude.

The fire started dying out, just as the sun began to rise. The glade slowly filled with pale sunshine.

Maude and Alex followed an overgrown path through the forest, stopping at a bubbling brook to get a drink. As Alex leaned over it, a very large dragonfly zoomed towards him, made a noisy circle around his head, and landed on a fern that bent over the water. Its wings were stiff and gauzy, and its body striped in metallic shades of blue, red and violet. In this forest where spiders talked and went to weddings, Alex was not sure of the proper thing to do.

"Hello," he said casually.

The dragonfly made a sputtering sort of buzz that might have been a laugh, and flew off dipping low over a blueberry patch on its way.

"Oh, good," said Alex, "something to eat," and he filled his handkerchief with berries. He offered some to Maude, but she refused with a slight smile indicating one or two parcels that hung beneath her cloak.

"I carry my own provisions," she explained.

In about an hour they reached the edge of the forest and saw a meadow filled with daisies and poppies before them. Among the flowers were many small grey figures resembling Maude. As they came closer, Alex saw that these spiders had woven the most fantastic webs with lovely patterns of snowflakes and butterflies. They were now putting these webs together and slowly forming the shape of a dress. They looked somehow tired and unhappy.

"Ah," breathed Maude. "The wedding gown is nearly ready." There was pride as well as sadness in her voice.

"Here's the veil," she announced to the gathering. "Let us roll them up together and carry them off to the tower. So much beautiful work for such an unhappy cause."

As she gestured, Alex saw a tall, dark building on a rocky outcropping in the distance. The sky around it was cloudy, and there was a sudden chill in the air as if it might snow.

Maude's bright eyes seemed to study Alex for a moment. "We have completed that monster's orders to save ourselves from death. Can you imagine a world without spiders? Mosquitoes and flies would rule the insect world and there would be no beautiful webs to catch the dewdrops and sparkle in the rain. But now that lovely young girl is to be sacrificed, and we can do nothing—unless . . ." her voice trailed off.

She waved an arm. "She's waiting for us over there."

Then she added very softly, "you may be the very hero mentioned in the old spell, the hero who saves the maiden with the help of the little grey people."

Alex paled. "How did she get here?" he asked.

"While looking for berries, she lost her way and was captured by Tarantella and his followers. She put up a brave fight, but could not escape," Maude said. "We spiders have no strength to set her free until, as the old spell says, the hero comes to help the grey ones.

"I was so happy to see you, Alex. If you are to be our hero, we must get you to the tower quickly or she will be doomed. You must not be seen, boy," she continued in a serious voice. "We grey ones would never hurt you, but," she added, "those others . . .

"Here, wear this," she took off her cloak and thrust it at him. Then he saw her plain grey face and plump body for the first time. Now that he knew her, she seemed both trustworthy and comforting.

"This is much too small," protested Alex as he placed her cape on his head, which it barely covered. Then, curiously, he seemed completely hidden under the cloak. He noticed that Maude's eight black eyes were staring directly into his as one hairy arm grasped him firmly.

"Come along now," she said in a rather bossy tone of voice and pushed him towards the others who had started off through the meadow. As he went on his reluctant way, he noticed that the flowers, which had grazed his ankle before, were now taller than he was.

"Why, I'm really small," he thought in alarm, "and there's something very nasty in that tower up ahead that could squash me with one big foot. But," he reassured himself, "it *is* an adventure and hopefully it will have a happy ending."

After some trudging through the tall grass and over small rocky hills, Maude murmured in his ear, "We are almost there. Keep covered." She pulled the grey hood closely about his face. "They aren't fond of boys here. Except for dinner," she added in an off-hand way.

Soon they arrived at the tower, which was made of large, rough rocks and closed by a rusty iron door. In front were many odd creatures swarming about, pushing and shoving and crawling over each other. They looked quite menacing, with shiny black armor on their backs and all sorts of strange knives and weapons tied onto their bodies. They wore round, black helmets with two long projecting feelers. Perhaps they were soldiers? Alex kept his head down. He did not wish to examine them too closely.

Maude conferred briskly with one at the main door, which was then opened. "Make way, make way for the royal wedding gown!" shouted a loud, rough voice.

 They were bustled up a worn, winding staircase covered in some places with slippery moss, leaves, and dirt. It was lit by narrow, glassless windows. The black, beetle-like things pushed, shoved and crowded behind them, clutching and climbing over each other's backs. Some of them lost a crooked leg or two, but no one seemed to care. Alex saw one drop a rusty sword. He grabbed it quickly and hid it under his cloak.

When they had reached the highest floor, they found themselves standing in front of a small door. A key was produced, and it opened the door with a loud creak.

The spiders moved forward and, as Alex peered in, he saw a small, dusty room lit by one long window. There was nothing in it except a three-paneled screen that stood in a corner.

"Stay here," Maude ordered Alex as he entered. She and the other spiders disappeared to the other side of the screen.

Alex noted uneasily that the black-armored guards were jostling about in the doorway. Faint moans and sobs could be heard from behind the screen. He edged near the window, the only possible means of escape, but the ground below seemed impossibly far away. His eyes circled the room and found, with a shiver, that there were creepy things in the corners such as you might find under an old rock. White, wormy shapes that had never seen the sun. As he turned around, the spiders came into view. In their midst was a girl dressed in the most beautiful clothes he had ever seen.

Her dress seemed to float on her as if made of fanciful moonbeams. Maude's lovely veil framed her face. Her golden hair hung long and free, but her pale face and blue eyes were filled with such sadness that his heart ached.

At that moment there was a great clashing and banging on the stairs outside and a roar of excited voices speaking in a strange language. One word was plain enough. "Tarantella," was shouted from one voice to another until through the door, in a burst of fetid air, came a terrifying figure.

Tarantella was much, much larger than any of the others. He, too, was dressed in black armor, but it was dented and cracked and streaked with brown. The dents and cracks seemed to be the scars of war and age. His gleaming, wicked eyes were buried in a furry face with strange bumps and pincers.

As this horrid being moved towards the spiders and the half-fainting princess, the soldiers swarmed behind him buzzing with excitement. The noise was deafening in that small room. As more and more insects crowded forward, Alex found himself pushed against Maude and the princess.

"Oh, someone help me," the princess cried faintly.

"My bride," answered Tarantella in a voice so creaky and harsh it seemed as if it had never been used. He stepped forward and placed his black claw upon the princess's frail wrist.

25

The window was just behind them. There was no other place to withdraw. Alex felt himself overwhelmed with loathing and fear.

"You're nothing but an enormous, disgusting bug!," he shouted in a fury, drawing his hidden sword. *"Disgusting,"* he repeated as loudly and clearly as possible to make sure that he was understood. Maude slipped a loop of silken web around his waist.

Tarantella came closer to view his bride, ignoring Alex, who must have seemed only a small, noisy spider. Alex saw instantly what needed to be done. He tied the web-rope tightly in a boy scout's knot and made another loop and knot around the princess' waist. Maude gave them an abrupt, hard shove towards the window.

"Jump!" she shouted in a voice of such conviction and command that they instantly leapt forward and hurtled outward through the air.

The wind blew away their screams as they seemed to fly from the tower supported by the threads of silvery cobwebs. They did not fall toward the ground but outward in a great arc, floating over the meadow and forest like two butterflies tossed in a storm until they gradually descended to land softly on a mossy bank.

Breathlessly, they stared at one another, happy to have escaped but astonished at the way in which it had happened. Here he was safe and sound and in a very familiar spot, Alex thought. They were by the edge of the very woods where he had sat while talking to the dragon. Was it only yesterday? And was that buzzing insect in front of him the same dragonfly that he had seen before? It looked familiar.

As for the princess, all that remained of her wedding gown were a few wisps that she brushed away, leaving an ordinary cotton dress. Alex, too, had changed into himself, having lost Maude's cape.

"She's just a little girl," thought Alex, looking into her tear-stained, dirty face.

"Are you really a princess?" he asked.

"My papa thinks so." She looked around her curiously. "Why, I'm close to home! There's the birch grove and the strawberry patch. I live over there." She pointed to the left along the edge of the woods. "I'd better hurry. They'll be worrying." She got up, dabbing at her cheeks with a small handkerchief that seemed to have been made by the spiders. She held out her hand shyly.

"Thank you, ever so much," she said formally. Then her face flushed and her eyes filled with fresh tears. "You and the spider lady saved my life," she added in a broken little voice. "Here," she pushed the handkerchief into his hand. "She made this, too. Keep it to remember me." She ran quickly away, looking back only once to wave goodbye.

"And to remember Maude," thought Alex. He looked up. Wasn't Aunt Rachel's house just over that hill? He hurried along and there it was with the apple tree beside it. Somehow it seemed a different time, early in the morning. Even the seagulls were quiet. Without a moment's thought, he mustered up the courage to climb the apple tree and push his way through the half-opened attic window.

"My first tree climb!" he thought.

He snuggled gratefully under the quilt, after placing the little lace handkerchief on the chest at the foot of his bed, and fell sound asleep.

The Third Day

hen Alex awoke, he had no idea of the time. It was dark and cool. Rain tapped against the window, which his Aunt had just shut. She stood, a dark cloth in hand, at the end of his bed.

"It's a dull day," she announced, "How about some pancakes to liven things up? Then you can play on the porch until it clears off. Cobwebs, everywhere," she muttered flicking her cloth about.

"Oh, no!" exclaimed Alex in distress as he watched the little lace handkerchief whisked off the chest. "I wanted to save that one."

"Save cobwebs?" said his Aunt, in surprise. "That's not easy to do. But, maybe," she laughed, taking a swipe at his head with her rag, "there are a few between your ears this morning. Let's go and eat."

Alex put on his old, blue sweater with the anchor on it and long pants. He hurried noisily down the stairs to the kitchen.

After breakfast, he looked at *National Geographic* while rocking in a wicker chair on the screened porch. Then he examined the sea shells lined up on the window ledges, a skeleton of a seahorse and dried starfish, small and large. Finally, he made a castle with colored paper and an oatmeal box and peopled it with some battered tin soldiers. He was beginning to feel bored when the screen door banged loudly. He looked up to see a very wet cat hanging and swinging on it. Little drops of water slid along its whiskers and its eyes were wide and pleading.

31

 He jumped to open the door. The cat scurried in dripping and jumped up on the rocking chair leaving a trail of muddy footprints. Alex wiped them up with the back of a sweater sleeve.

"Well, look who's here," said his Aunt's voice just behind him, "Daisy."

Alex looked carefully, and saw that the cat was marked in black, white, and orange like a tiger. A large black patch on her back had a white, star-shaped spot with an orange center on it. It *did* look like a daisy.

"I didn't know you had a cat," said Alex. He smiled and patted her gently. When he put his head down near hers, she gave him a quick, rough lick on the forehead.

"Oh, she's not *my* cat," said Aunt Rachel, laughing. "She's nobody's cat and everybody's cat. She travels around from house to house and is always welcome to stay. She's very independent, our Daisy, and we are honored by her visits.

"Looks like you've found yourself a friend," said his Aunt with satisfaction. "Maybe Daisy will share a tuna fish sandwich with you for lunch. And then a nap might be in order. It's clearing up and we can go the Firemen's Carnival tonight."

As they all ate, Aunt Rachel described the prizes they might win and the rides they could take. "There's a funhouse, too," she declared. "All mirrors! We'll see how fast you can escape."

She sent him upstairs for the quilt and lit a fire in the fireplace. "Too soon to start the furnace, so this will take the dampness out," she said. "Just curl up in that big chair."

Daisy jumped up too and snuggled down on the quilt. Her paw, Alex noticed as he yawned loudly, was just touching a patch of blue-green with strings of tiny dots like pearls or bubbles spattered across it.

omehow, he and Daisy had arrived at the beach, although he could not remember walking there. The rain had cleared off, and the setting sun lit the edges of the long, grey clouds with gold. There was a salty tang in the air. At his feet was a large tidal pool filled with dark seaweed. As he watched, snail shells with dainty crab's feet skittered into the water. Daisy was at his side in an instant, eyes filled with a curious, green light. Her sharp, white teeth gleamed in her pink mouth. Around her waist, he was surprised to see a slender black belt with a small, silver dagger tucked into it. All of a sudden, the pool rose up to their ankles, then their waists, and then they were suddenly and terrifyingly sucked beneath its surface in one great gulp.

Alex was quite a good swimmer, but he could not make a single stroke as they were dragged along by a tremendous current deep into the ocean. Ahead of him he could just see Daisy's small body twisting and turning. Her mouth was clamped shut, but her eyes were wide open.

"I can't breathe," thought Alex in terror. Then they hit the sandy bottom and he took a gasping, shuddering breath. They were drifting effortlessly in calm water lit by shafts of green sunlight from far above. He and Daisy were not far from a coral reef. Certainly there was not one to be found in the sea near his Aunt's house. Stranger still, they both seemed able to breathe naturally.

"What shall we do?" shouted Alex in a funny, bubbling voice as he caught up to the cat.

"Have a bit of excitement, I suppose," Daisy answered coolly. Her eyes had a wild spark in them, and she seemed to have acquired a gold earring. Her white paws trod the water gracefully as she kicked her strong back legs. "Oh, look," she added with a slightly growling accent, "Fish! Fish *everywhere!*"

Small schools of red and yellow fish flickered around the coral. There were black and white striped fish and funny, puffed fish with spines. There were even rainbow-colored fish sleeping in sacs of clear goo. Daisy suddenly disappeared in a great splash of sand and water, and Alex shrieked in fear.

She returned shortly, wiping her little dagger on a piece of seaweed and licking the corners of her mouth. "Not bad, not bad at all," she pronounced while tiny, silver bubbles spun around her head like soda pop.

This all seemed so very odd that Alex lost his fear and regained his curiosity. He started to explore. He avoided the purple sea urchins because of their spines but watched a striped fish squirt one with water to turn it over and avoid being pricked. He saw a sea star eating an oyster with relish.

"Everything is eating everything else," he thought with a shiver, and when he was rudely bumped by a brown fish four times his size, he hid behind a giant clam shell.

Shortly afterwards he heard Daisy calling him.

"Come on, this way," she shouted, "I see a cave."

"A cave," thought Alex, "is that good?" but he followed her just the same—and in a hurry, as if he were going to a lovely party.

The cave was of dull bluestone and apparently empty except for a lot of tube-like shapes hanging on lines like wash across its ceiling. These clotheslines were fastened at one end to three nails with golden tips and at the other to some coral branches growing high up on the cave's wall.

"Are these someone's little stockings?" Alex wondered. "But how do clothes get dry down here?"

He was just beginning to imagine the sort of creature with many legs that might wear such things, when he noticed two bright, black spots in the rear of the cave that seemed to blink. Could they be eyes?

"Hello, anybody home?" Daisy inquired noisily rapping at the cave's entrance with the hilt of her knife. In fascination Alex saw the eyes being joined by a reddish, plump body and eight waving arms.

"An octopus," Alex thought, and his heart gave a skip. "But not a very big one," and he was grateful for that. Then he looked directly into those dark, soft eyes with thin, heavy lids. They looked so human and so gentle that he felt no fear at all.

"Oh dear, visitors," said a fussy, small voice. "And not a drop of food to offer them." The octopus waved her tentacles in agitation and flushed redder still. "I haven't had a bite to eat in days myself," she quavered and paled to orange. "I've been watching my eggs, you see." She blew out a string of bubbles and gently stroked and cleaned the dangling objects that Alex had mistaken for stockings.

"Ah," said Daisy, quickly in a voice of exaggerated sweetness. "You are to be a mother, and these are your kittens. A mother needs food to take care of her little ones." Abruptly, she swam off into the seaweed and, such were her hunting skills, that she returned speedily with a number of shrimp clutched to her chest. She offered several to the octopus mother and ate two herself.

"How kind," murmured the octopus shyly, turning pink.

"Shrimp are delicious," Daisy replied. "Delicious," she repeated in a hissing cat-like way. "And your little eggs will soon hatch into delicious—"

"Daisy, stop!" said Alex severely. "Do you happen to know the way back to the tidal pool?" he asked, as much to change the subject as to find the answer. "We're lost."

"Ask Father Neptune," the octopus replied after shutting her eyes to think, "he's sure to know but he's in a very bad mood since his trident disappeared. He's just over that way," she gestured vaguely with her many arms.

They swam into a strong current as they waved goodbye and were carried along quite easily until they came to a dense mass of pale green seaweed that slowed them to a halt. Tiny snails and crabs and bits of red coral clung to it, and trails of bubbles twisted around its strands like chains of pearls. It waved and swayed in front of them, a moving wall. Daisy drew her knife and stabbed and cut at it violently to make a pathway.

Just then, a huge, glittering fish tail slapped down in a spray of foam, nearly hitting them, and a thunderous voice shouted, "Stop!"

They looked upwards towards the stream of bursting bubbles that accompanied this noise and saw, far above, a pale face hovering in the water. Its mouth was a dark cave-like hole, its nose large and its eyes blue and popping. "Stop!" the deep voice repeated, and the sea bottom seemed to shake.

"Come here, you misbegotten imps," shouted the voice.

Clinging together, Alex and Daisy rose through the dappled currents until they were level with Father Neptune (Alex recognized him instantly from the pictures he had seen in old books). He was wearing a golden crown embedded with pearls. His long, green beard covered most of his body, but his face was quite nice upon a closer look. With his pink nose and cheeks, he was like an underwater Santa Claus.

"We're lost," yelled Alex, "sir," he added more gently. "We were in a tidal pool and got dragged down here. We want to go home now." He felt the tears rise into his eyes, but no one could see them where everything was wet.

Father Neptune's mossy eyebrows drew down into a frown. "I've lost my trident, boy," he answered crossly, "and no one's going anywhere until I find it. You must have been sucked down here when I dropped it. It controls the tides, storms, and earthquakes, you see. Not much fun without it! No excitement, nothing to look forward to—" he shook his head in despair, and his mouth took a downward turn.

"Well, we have to go home," said Daisy suddenly. "Or we'll

turn into fish and . . ." she stopped suddenly and took a deep breath. "Not that it would be a *bad* thing, mind you. What if we found your  trident," she offered hopefully, "could we go back then?"

Neptune's eyebrows rose in surprise. "Of course," he said delightedly. "What a good idea! Fresh point of view and all that . . ." He clapped his hands suddenly. "And Hector can help you. Just hold onto his bridle, and you'll go much faster and return faster too— with my trident!"

A very large seahorse, at least three feet tall, appeared suddenly. This was Hector. His coloring was brilliant—red, blue, and violet metallic colors flowing into ridges and scallops down his neck. He had a long tail upon which he balanced himself gracefully, fluttering his fins. Around his nose, or snout, and his head were bands of woven sea grass ending in a bridle. Alex was quite struck by the seahorse's appearance, especially since there seemed to be something curiously familiar about him.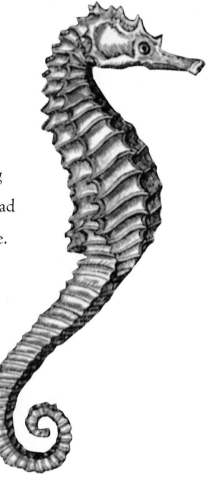

"Haven't we met before?" Alex asked hesitatingly, "You seem to remind me . . ."

"Of a cousin?" said the seahorse

quickly, "an uncle who has passed away? We all have our doubles, they say," he added in a rather silly way, swiveling his eyes about, one searching the water above and the other the sand below, as if looking for this elusive twin. "But," he tossed his head, and the bridle fell into Alex's hand, "we had best be off!"

Alex had just enough time to grab Daisy and tuck her firmly under his arm. They sped away at a dizzying pace, winding at top speed through swaying forests of seaweed and deep purple caverns. They startled a huge round fish that hung like a fallen sun in the water, and once had to hide from a sleek, sinister shape that swam far above them. It had a receding chin and a large fin like a small snail. "Please, not a shark," Alex begged silently, but it was.

After what seemed like a very long time and without any sign of a trident, Daisy began to wriggle violently. She struck the seahorse lightly with the hilt of her knife and meowed. They came to a halt.

"Enough," she hissed. "It's time to eat; I'm starved." She disappeared in pursuit of some small fish hiding in a blue sponge. Alex looked around. "We're back at the coral reef," he thought. "We must have traveled for miles, and we're right back where we started from!"

"How can we ever find that trident?" he asked aloud. "We'll be down here forever," he said in a rather weepy voice, which the seahorse seemed not to notice. Daisy was certainly in a better mood when she returned, but Alex was quite downhearted.

"We'll turn into fish," he said sadly.

"Well, I've heard of catfish," replied Daisy in a brisk voice, "but never boyfish. Of course, there's a first time for everything," she added, winking at the seahorse.

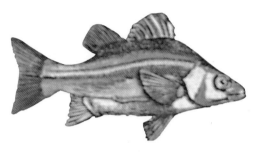

"It's no joke," said Alex desperately, "I want to go home."

"To Aunty Em," said Daisy, trying to be funny, "just click your heels together three times and . . ."

"I'm sure if we look just a little further," the seahorse interrupted kindly. "Isn't there a cave around here?" He looked around tossing his head and widening his eyes in a theatrical way. In no time they found the octopus's cave and the octopus herself, waving her tentacles gently and looking very tired. Her soft, dark eyes glowed at seeing them again. She had been taking care of her eggs for days with no rest and seemed quite pale.

Daisy produced some small crabs, which the octopus gratefully accepted.

"Ah, the little ones are all strung up on these clotheslines," said the seahorse, rolling his eyes madly. "Just look, three lines fastened to three golden nails on this side and to three coral branches on the other. How very artistic," he burbled. "Where did you find three golden nails, Madam?"

"I found them lying in the sand," the octopus answered dreamily, the faintest flush of pink deepening beneath her eyes.

"They were fastened to a thin bar and I saw instantly, *instantly*," she repeated, "how such a thing might be used."

"How very clever," the seahorse replied with a sharp intake of breath, moving closer and closer to the clothesline. "See the three . . . prongs, might one call them? Look Alex, look Daisy. Three curved prongs—you see they are actually curved—on a bar. Now what does that remind you of?" he finished in a loud, clear voice.

"He sounds exactly like a teacher who already knows the answer," thought Alex barely listening. But Daisy's green eyes flew wide open.

"It's the trident!" she screamed.

"Indeed," said the seahorse with something as close to a smile as a seahorse can achieve.

"And now," he quickly removed his bridle and tied it securely to the clothesline and around an outcropping of rock that held the line up, "we will simply fix it so . . . the eggs will be safe this way." He then pulled out the trident and held it firmly in his mouth.

"Are you ready?"

"Yes," Alex and Daisy replied breathlessly.

Hector struck the trident hard against the

sandy bottom and there was a violent shake and hiss of bubbles.

"Goodbye," they heard faintly, as they burst like rockets through the water.

"Goodbye," murmured Alex sleepily as he awoke in the soft chair before the fire. Daisy was licking his face, and he was not surprised to feel that her whiskers were rather wet.

The Fourth Night

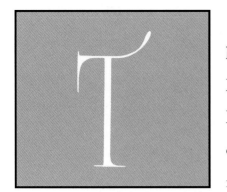he next day had passed happily. Alex had quickly learned that the beach was a good place to play. He smoothed the sand down and with big stones outlined a long, wiggly shape, decorating the inside with shells and pebbles. A piece of brown beach glass made a wonderful eye. When he was done, Alex was not at all surprised to see that he had made the image of a large dragon.

Washed up on the sand were small, dried starfish that he could imagine on a Christmas tree. Even the bayberries that grew along the beach, Aunt Rachel had said, could be boiled into wax and made into candles.

Alex was sitting on a rock eating the peanut butter sandwich he had made for lunch, when Daisy arrived to share the container of milk he had brought.

"Just imagine, Daisy," said Alex, pouring a little milk into an old clam shell for her, "kids long ago made things just like these. They didn't go to a toy store, they *imagined* their fun."

"Of course," he added, laughing, "they didn't have milk cartons, just cows." He patted Daisy and tickled her whiskers, feeling a little sad that his week was going by so quickly. Maybe Aunt Rachel would come and visit him for Christmas and see the little starfish hanging on his tree.

That night Alex lay on his bed in his blue pajamas beside the sleeping Daisy. He was remembering the carnival, the bright colored lights and the loud music of the night before. Best of all had been the funhouse where nothing was as it seemed, and the glass walls reflected everything but the way out. It was so late when they got home, sticky with taffy-apples and spun sugar candy that he had fallen into a dreamless sleep. But tonight, when Daisy curled her toes and opened one green eye to stare at him, he felt a shiver of excitement.

"Which one, Daisy?" he whispered.

She stretched out a paw to touch a square smeared roughly with many colors as if someone had used it to wipe off paint brushes.

"Ah, Daisy," murmured Alex doubtfully, but, before he had time to object, his eyes had closed and he seemed to whirl away in a spangle of stardust.

He was sitting on the top ledge of a number of stone slabs that were stuck unevenly into the slope of a hill as steps. Between these rocks were ferns and moss and little brown mushroom caps. It was a fair day, and down below him in a small grotto stood two people, a young man and a woman, busily painting a make-believe tree. As Alex leaned forward to take a closer look, his hand slipped down the wet, rocky wall, that half-enclosed the space where the two stood. He looked, and was surprised to find his hand covered with paint.

"Well, that's done," he heard the young man say, putting his paint brush into an empty pot and stepping back to admire his work. "It will just need a lantern or two up there," he gestured at the tree, "and masses of candles over there," pointing towards the rock wall and what appeared to be a dark opening in its surface, "to catch Sir Hugo going up against the hideous dragon."

"Hideous?" a voice queried from above, "am I to wear make-up then?"

Alex saw instantly that the voice came from his old friend, the dragon, who sat halfway down the rocky stairs swinging his clawed feet back and forth over the wall's edge. He held his pipe in one hand and a plume of smoke drifted upwards as he contemplated the workers below.

Alex coughed, and the dragon turned his head.

"Coming to the show tonight?" the dragon inquired pleasantly. "We're giving the usual yearly play to keep the townspeople amused."

"Oh, it's so good to see you, dragon," cried Alex in delight. "What is this place, anyway?" Then he suddenly became unhappily aware that the dragon didn't know him.

"Don't you remember me?" he asked in a voice of disbelief. He rose and walked down the stairs to look into his friend's face.

The dragon's nut-brown eyes stared at him blankly. He waved

his paw about as if at a loss for words.

"I meet so many admirers," he smirked. "The theater life, you know. Of course," he leaned forward and crinkled his eyes into a smile, "I'm glad you think of me as a friend; it warms this old actor's heart."

Alex felt very cross.

"Could the dragon be pretending?" he wondered. Then out from some leafy bushes a small, agile figure bounded forward and curled itself around his leg.

"Daisy!" he knelt down, and she leapt upon his shoulder, purring noisily and rubbing her face against his head. He squeezed his eyes shut for an instant and felt a warm feeling in his chest. At least he had one good friend present.

"What a darling kitty," said the young woman below brightly. She was both tall and sturdy with a frizzy red ponytail and freckles. "May I pet her?"

Alex felt Daisy hiss slightly in his ear, but he carried her down into the grotto and put her on the ground.

"Oh, dear little Puss, I do love animals so," she said, gazing at Daisy tenderly and kneeling to stroke her fur.

The young man coughed in an interrupting way. "We'd best get back to try on your costume, Elspeth?"

"Oh, yes, Giles," she sighed, rising. "I'm sure it will be lovely. White satin, you said? I will wear it when Hugo and I are wed," she added dreamily. "Both in the play, and I hope in real life too," she blushed.

She smiled warmly at Giles, patting his brown cheek in an off-handed way. "You've made it all possible," she cooed, "dear Giles."

As she turned away to collect the other paint jars, Alex saw a look of complete misery on Giles's face. He was all brown, Alex noted. Brown hair, brown eyes, a brown smock, and brown, wrinkled tights. The only other colors were from daubs left from painting, one blue splash amusingly striping his long, brown nose.

Watching the unhappy Giles, Alex thought "Even if it is only a play, he certainly doesn't seem to like the idea of Elspeth and Hugo being a couple."

"We'll see you at eight o'clock sharp," Giles called up to the dragon. "We've got lots of buckets of fake blood behind the cave wall. I know it will be the best show yet." He nodded at Alex and trudged after Elspeth.

Looking after them, Alex saw the spires of a castle rising behind some trees. He bent down to whisper in Daisy's ear,

"Let's go see the castle." Staring coolly back at the dragon, who waved languidly, he called, "See you later."

Now, if ever, was the moment for the dragon to acknowledge him. There was no one around to see. But the dragon carelessly crossed his legs and leaned back, shutting his eyes to rest.

"Couldn't care less . . ." repeated Alex angrily. "What kind of a friend is that?"

Daisy bounded ahead of him for some distance then, looking back, noticed that his bare feet were slowing him down.

"Wait," she said briefly and disappeared into the woods where some thatched roofs could be seen.

"Where did you get these?" said Alex disapprovingly, as she reappeared suddenly dragging a pair of short leather boots, one of which held a stout belt.

"Just found them lying around," answered Daisy, wide-eyed. "Put them on."

Alex, booted and belted in his blue pajamas, didn't look at all out of place as they encountered farmers and townspeople streaming towards a marketplace just outside the city walls. There was a man selling bread and cheese who handed Alex a filled roll when he saw the hungry boy. Daisy, too, came back from a little exploration smelling strongly of sausage.

No one paid attention to Daisy as her sharp ears picked up all the news. Alex waited for her sitting against the low wall that enclosed the castle moat. She finally crawled into his lap and settled down.

"Well," said Daisy, "the big performance is tonight, of course, 'The Slaying of the Dragon by Sir Hugo.'"

"Slaying?" hiccupped Alex, re-tasting the garlic cheese he had just eaten. "You don't mean killing? Why would anyone?. . ."

"Oh, it's not real," purred Daisy. "It's just 'pretend-to-be.' It used to be real in the old days. They would leave some poor maiden tied to a tree, and the dragon would come and eat her."

Alex knit his brow. "I can't imagine this dragon . . ." he began.

"Then," continued Daisy, "a brave knight would save her just in the nick of time. He'd charge up on his horse and stab the dragon to death." Her eyes glowed, and her pink tongue flickered in enjoyment. "I wouldn't want to miss it, would you? Everyone is going."

Alex felt a little uneasy when he thought of the dragon but surely it was all in fun. Wasn't that girl who so loved animals going to be the maiden?

"Then later," added Daisy as if reading his thoughts, "that big, red-headed creature will marry Sir Hugo, and there will be a huge party and lots to eat and drink. They do it every year to amuse the poor workers. Different maidens and knights, of course, and different dragons too, I suppose, or people would know it wasn't real."

"They think it's real?" questioned Alex, "but it's all so fake and a painted scene and make-believe blood! He's a really good painter, of course," he then mused. "I've never seen any-thing so perfect, and it's fun to pretend that dragons are terrible and eat people.

"Well," he hugged Daisy, "we'll go. Look at the sky, it will get dark soon. I don't know if we can find a seat, but maybe we can help and get to see it all that way."

As the first silver star appeared, the castle's gates swung open and there was an ominous sound of slowly beaten drums.

Boom, boom, boom!

The crowd gasped and parted. There were a number of sobs and groans. Some women put their hands over their mouths as if to stifle cries and men bowed their heads. Boom, boom, boom!

Between rows of lit candles, held in the hands of grim, cowled figures, came the maiden Elspeth. Alex held up Daisy to see. Could that beauty really be Elspeth? Her long, white dress gleamed in the candlelight, while her red hair, braided with pearls, hung long on either side of her pale face. Her eyes were almost shut, and the lids touched with the merest bit of blue paint. Winding around her wrists and waist was a golden chain that fell almost to the ground. There were tears from the audience, as the people fell in behind her. Alex saw Giles among them, his face as desolate as if the play were all real. He ran after him carrying Daisy.

"Can we stay with you?" Alex gently asked him.

"Well, I'll be busy, of course," said
Giles gloomily, "but you could help with
the blood," he brightened. "You could be
my assistant."

As they arrived at the grotto, Alex
was directed where to stand. It was all paint and imagination, he discovered, even the cave wasn't real. The dragon stood between two tall
boards, artfully designed, ready to make his entrance.

"Come to help?" said the dragon, rubbing his paws together,
"good audience," he jabbered nervously, peeking out. There was a low
drum roll, and the lights came on as if by magic.

Elspeth stood fastened to the painted tree by the golden chain.
Her head was thrown back, eyes shut, and her mouth open in an
expression of extreme suffering.

"No, no," she murmured brokenly, "save me, save poor
Elspeth from the dragon."

There was a sudden explosion of sound, a great rumbling,
snorting roar and a flicker of flame burst from the "cave" as an acrid
smoke filled the air. The audience screamed wildly and holding hands
over ears, raced for higher ground.

"A lot of good they'd do if it were real," grumbled Alex,
standing by the buckets of blood with which he was to douse the
dragon at a signal from Giles.

Elspeth's head drooped as if the full horror of her situation had become apparent. Her body sagged gracefully against the tree.

As the dragon roared again and started to creep from the cave, a mailed and helmeted figure appeared on an awkward-looking white horse. The figure came to a halt to assess the situation. The plumed head of Sir Hugo, for it was indeed he, nodded at Elspeth, and his plump belly swung forward as he lowered his lance.

"Foul dragon," he shrieked dramatically, through his large moustache, drooping like squirrel's tails on either side of his mouth, "prepare to die!"

Elspeth's eyes opened wide and she panted in great, shuddering breaths. The dragon, billowing smoke, rushed forward.

"Ouch!" he yelled loudly as the horse clumsily trod upon his toes. "Watch out you—no-o-o-o!" At that instant, Sir Hugo's spear struck him hard upon the shoulder and he fell backwards.

Alex was about to spill the blood when he saw it was not needed. The dragon was bleeding quite enough.

"Oh, you idiot," cried Elspeth, having escaped her chains, glaring at Sir Hugo. "Look what you've done. Poor, poor, dragon," she crooned, ripping off the bottom part of her white gown and stanching the blood as she knelt by his side.

"Cobwebs and milkweed," she ordered and Daisy rushed off to get them. "Then a nice, warm herbal tea. There, there, we'll take care of you."

Giles was by her side as Elspeth applied the cobwebs and milkweed juice and firmly bandaged the injured dragon's shoulder. Giles removed his tunic and fashioned a sling.

Sir Hugo wandered off, hanging his silly head in embarrassment.

The audience watched these events open-mouthed. They then began to think that this was a new, modern retelling of the old dragon story. The terrible, fire-belching dragon of earlier days was now a helpless victim, and the heroic knight of before was a clumsy fool. Worst of all, Elspeth's face had clearly shown her dislike and disappointment.

A great murmur rose from the crowd.

"What utter rot!" could be heard.

"Give us back our hero!" was shouted.

"You call *this* entertainment?" A shower of pinecones, hastily scooped up from the ground, was hurled upon the actors.

Alex saw the angry mob grow closer yelling: "get the dragon!" He feared for his friend. He rushed to the back of the scenery and grabbed the buckets of red paint, one in each hand. He spun wildly, spattering their wet-redness over all the candles that lit the stage. They sputtered out leaving the scene almost completely dark, except for the moon, which shone fitfully upon a horrid vision of blood-soaked trees and the body of a limp dragon.

There was a sudden hush and then a terrible gargling howl. The audience gasped in horror. The hair-raising cry from the bloody scene below filled them with mindless terror. They broke and ran.

Daisy raised her nose moonward once again and cried like a lost spirit.

"There, that ought to do it," she murmured.

Alex squatted on his heels by the dragon's head and petted him gently.

"After all, he is my friend," he thought. "He just couldn't remember me for a moment."

Alex, Elspeth, and Giles carried the dragon back by the make-believe cave after first making a great, soft pile of leaves and ferns for his bed. His eyes rolled weakly in his head, and he looked at Alex in a puzzled sort of way.

"You *are* a friend, aren't you," he said faintly.

"Just drink this," said Elspeth briskly, "and you'll get some sleep." She poured a yellow liquid down his throat, and his eyes shut.

She turned to Giles, "You've been marvelous," she said, clutching his shoulder. "Next time we'll get it right. This fantastic scenery won't go to waste, you'll see. Next time you should play the hero."

"You'll stay with our dear dragon?" she inquired of Alex and

Daisy. "We'll be back first thing in the morning," as she drew Giles away.

They started off on their way back to the castle, arms around each other's waists. There was a look of bright happiness on Giles's face.

Elspeth looked at him with wide eyes and suddenly smiled.

Daisy's green eyes shone and her pink mouth curved. "Looks like the wedding's off," she noted.

She curled up beside the sleeping dragon and so did Alex, until the morning sun and empty stomachs awakened them at Aunt Rachel's house. The dragon slept on, however. He was not to awaken until several hundred years had passed, in a pile of leaves in quite another place.

The Fifth Night

aisy had been with Alex all afternoon. She had been hiding and jumping like a jungle beast out of the stiff, brown grass by the edge of the brook. Alex had made a splendid dam with interwoven sticks, stones, and a smooth, muddy side over which the water spilled on its way down to the beach.

Daisy had just discovered a small crayfish hiding under a rock when Alex called to her hurriedly. "Come!" he said, clapping his hands together sharply. "It's getting late. I'll race you to the hill."

Happily distracted, Daisy took great leaps, her belly close to the ground and her ears laid back. She sat on the back steps waiting until Alex arrived, puffing like the big, bad wolf.

"Well, here you are," said Aunt Rachel opening the door. "You must be starved. Open that tuna fish for our guest, Alex. I've had the soup kettle on all day, and there's some good, homemade bread for cheese sandwiches."

To Alex food had never tasted so good.

"It's all that fresh sea air," explained his Aunt.

After they finished supper, Alex and Daisy lay in front of the fireplace reading very old comic books. At least Daisy *seemed* to be reading. Perhaps she was just scratching her chin on the edge of the book. A little later, yawning, they went upstairs, and Daisy lay across the bed like a fur scarf. Completely relaxed, she hardly seemed to breathe but, now and then, her paws would curl and twitch, and she would make faint moans. One paw, Alex noticed, lay upon a patch of purple triangles rising to a dark sky with clouds. He put his head down near hers and saw green with bits of brown and something that might have been a violet.

☽

His head rested upon soft moss and all around him were little patches of brown mushrooms, piles of pinecones and acorn caps, baby ferns and violets intermingled with white pebbles and sand. It was almost like a living patchwork quilt, he thought confusedly. Where was he? Something lightly tickled his cheek, and he raised his head to see a line of light, shiny, black eyes staring at him fixedly.

"Maude!"

"Yes," said the familiar, whispery voice.

"You escaped!"

Maude gave a dry chuckle. Her plain grey face almost seemed  to smile as she lifted a furry foreleg to touch his face. "You've come just in time to help us again," she said quietly but with a firmness that sent a slight shiver down his back.

Alex sat up and became suddenly aware that they were not alone. Two brown rabbits, nervously twitching thin pink noses, stared at him with wide brown eyes. A squirrel, head-down-wards on a nearby tree, chattered and flicked its tail. Several wood mice stood near Maude, wearing acorn helmets and carrying sharpened sticks as lances. As he turned his head, a mole with fur like velvet popped out of a hole in the ground. It pointed its sharp nose here and there, and with one of its big front paws pulled out some wire-rimmed glasses to peer through.

"Ah, there you all are," it squeaked. "Has the meeting begun?"

"We're all here," cried a chipmunk, racing up with several others.

"Where's Daisy?" Alex suddenly wondered, missing her.

"She went to the next square to wait for you," replied Maude. "For several reasons," she added, looking quite pointedly at the mice and the elegant mole, "we thought it best."

He was very fond of Daisy, Alex thought, but sometimes she was not quite dependable. "Being free," she called it but sometimes it was just "being naughty."

"This is Alex, of course?" one of the rabbits piped up.

"Yes," said Maude, settling down on top of the large mossy stone. "Our dragon friend thought that Alex could help us. He felt that he, himself, would cause far too much attention in these small woods. He even said that, in fact, no one believed in dragons or their ancient wisdom anymore. It was quite sad."

"Oh, I do," said Alex passionately. "I know the dragon, person-ally, and he knows me. At least, most of the time," he mumbled

65

uneasily. "But he wanted me to come and help?" he added in a relieved tone after a second's thought, "and here I am."

"Of course," murmured Maude soothingly. "We know you can help us, dear Alex. Some would say it was a very small adventure, but it does mean the lives of many of us here."

Alex stared at her, round-eyed, but he remembered the young princess and a feeling of bravery swelled his chest.

"Of course I will help," he said looking at all the small creatures warmly. "What can I do?"

"It's the poachers!" they all cried at once, "the martens and the weasels. They've left the big forest and come to prey on us."

"They sell our furs," chattered a rabbit holding his paws across his chest as if to quiet his rapid heart.

"They trap and kill," said the mole mournfully, blowing his nose, "no one is safe. One after another, our loved ones disappear."

"To reappear as 'lucky' rabbit's feet at the county fair or as a squirrel's tail without its owner, decorating a bicycle," said the squirrel, shaking so with emotion that he could hardly speak.

"This must cease," said Maude's firm voice. "And it will," she looked at Alex expectantly.

"Yes," responded Alex nobly. "I will do it." But, what was to be done? He rested his back against the rock where Maude sat and frowned in concentration.

The animals stood in a ring, waiting.

"What *are* poachers?" he finally asked.

"They catch animals in traps, skin them, and sell their fur."

"Aha," said Alex, and thought some more.

"Well, we must catch them first!" he burst out triumphantly.

There was excited chittering and squeaking.

A sudden, dark shadow passed across the wooded area, and the air grew chill. Looking up, Alex saw a large owl flying high above. When he looked down again, all the little furred creatures had disappeared. Only Maude remained.

"An enemy spy," she said briefly. "We must go to Bettina's for the night. I'll leave a note for the rest."

She draped a cobweb over the rock filled with tiny, crooked letters. Alex stretched his legs and followed her through the dusky woods until they arrived at a small, tumbled-down, cottage under a pine tree. There was a flickering light inside, and the door opened at Maude's knock.

"Come in, come in," said a welcoming voice.

So this was Bettina, Alex thought, and Bettina was—a what? She looked like a dumpy witch in a fairy-tale book with her pointed hat and lacy shawl, but her hands were black and furry, and her whiskered nose was black too. A broad, white band came down her brow and ended between her merry, brown eyes. As she turned, Alex noticed that beneath her skirt a large tail curved. It was striped in white, too.

"I hope we didn't startle you," Alex asked politely as he and Maude entered the small house.

"Startle me?" Bettina answered in amused surprise. "Oh, no, it's usually quite the other way around," she giggled, giving Maude a quick, side-long glance.

They sat around an iron stove eating roasted chestnuts and drinking cider.

"We've come for your help," said Maude finally, sighing contentedly. "Alex is making plans, and we hope to get rid of those dreadful poachers once and for all. We all know what a contribution you can make."

"A contribution, indeed," replied Bettina laughing heartily. "Is that what you call it? Well, they're no friends of mine. I'll do what I can," she smirked at Alex knowingly, but he couldn't imagine why and lamely thanked her for the delicious food.

"Spending the night?" she then asked, and Maude nodded her head. At that very instant, there was a shrill and sudden scream from the darkened woods.

"Quick!" shouted Bettina, grabbing a large, brilliantly orange mushroom which glowed in the dark as they raced into the night.

69

"This way," called Bettina flashing her mushroom light. She seemed to hear something with her sharp ears.

The moon slid out from behind a cloud and revealed the sad figure of a rabbit, hanging upside down, his foot caught in a loop of rope. He was kicking weakly. Beneath him, a second rabbit, panting in terror, sprang wildly.

Alex's heart leapt in his throat. He reacted instantly, reaching up to loosen the noose and gently release the captive.

"You'll be all right, now," he said, rubbing the bruised leg.

Bettina took a small bottle from her pocket and urged the rabbits to take a sip. They did, but in a humble, cautious way. "They're a little wary," thought Alex. "Of course . . . they were very frightened."

"Off you go now," said Maude as the rabbits scampered off. "Go straight home. We'll be at Bettina's making plans for tomorrow."

"Plans?" thought Alex blankly. "Oh, yes, I must think of something." But when they arrived back at the cottage, his mind felt duller and duller and he fell sound asleep in front of the warm fire.

He awoke, somewhat stiff from lying on the floor, not remembering where he was. He tried to find Daisy, but she wasn't there, nor was anyone else. The small room, filled with the grey light of early morning, was completely empty. He rubbed his eyes and sat up. There was a strange, empty feeling in his stomach.

He remembered the animals. What was he going to do? It all came back in a rush of despair. His eyes scanned the room as if he might find an answer there, but they only found a cup of luke-warm tea and a blueberry tart placed upon a nearby stool where he could find them. He ate quickly, for he was hungry. Then he felt a little better.

"What would the dragon do?" he mused. "He seemed so old and so wise." And, as if the dragon himself had answered, an idea came suddenly into his head.

"A trap!" he thought, and he knew exactly how to do it. As if on cue, the door opened, and Maude entered briskly.

"It's a bit drizzly out," she said.

"All the better," answered Alex cheerfully. "Are you ready to get the poachers?"

"Oh, Alex," said Maude in delight, "I knew you could do it! The others are all waiting down at the big rock. Bettina will be there, too."

It was a busy morning. First the mole and several of his broth-ers, using their large front paws like shovels, dug very deep, narrow holes. They almost seemed to swim through the ground. Then all the animals formed lines from the holes to where a brook gurgled its way through the woods. All sorts of pots and pans were put to use, filled with water, passed paw to paw,

 and dumped into the excavations. The squirrels busily smoothed the wet soil into dripping, slippery slopes while the fine misty rain helped to keep them damp. Chipmunks and mice rushed to pull branches and moss over the openings. Cleverly they added mushrooms, grass and pebbles until the trap was perfectly disguised and looked just like the ground around them.

Maude and Bettina, her hat decorated with a bunch of violets, watched in anticipation.

"Oh, it's sure to work," said Maude happily, then added with a quick note of fear, "but you, Alex, must be very careful. They'll remember you. You're a boy and different."

As the late afternoon shadows striped the ground, the rabbits began the final part of the plan.

They staggered across the ground as if they were ill or wounded. Their ears hung down forlornly, and their eyes were glazed and dull. With panting breaths, they dragged their back legs as if they were barely able to walk. Alex and the others hid and watched. No movement or sound was to be heard but that of the "injured" rabbits wavering near the hidden holes. A dark shadow passed high in the sky duplicating itself on the ground. A low whistle was heard and quickly as a striking snake, out from the trees they came. Animals, fierce and agile, with mouths pulled back from sharp teeth and evil, slanting eyes. The rabbits, quivering, heroically stood on the far side of each hole. The poaching weasels and martens, running to attack, plunged through the slender sticks and moss, sliding down, down, as if into a deep well. Scrambling and pawing at slippery, muddy sides, they could hear the great cheer that went up, and for the first time felt afraid.

The rabbits were embraced, patted on the back and carried on the others' shoulders in a triumphant parade. Their shy grins were charmingly accented by their big front teeth. It was then that Bettina, her violets nodding, stood over each hole and committed the final insult.

"There, you nasty beasts," she shouted. "When you escape, go home and let us never see your ugly faces again!"

A strange, pungent odor could be sniffed on the air. Bettina was, Alex suddenly realized, a skunk, and she had sprayed the poachers with a terrible smell. He laughed until tears clouded his eyes and his throat hurt.

He heard Maude calling him and felt her urgently tugging at his clothes. Small paws pushed at his legs, and there was a sudden hush in the celebration. As he rubbed his eyes, he felt a powerful rush of wind above his head and saw something large and orange like a small bright sun in the sky, or was it—an eye! He stared up into the eyes of a huge owl, wings outstretched, and cruel beak open.

They all stood on the edge of a small hill, and Alex swayed as desperate little animals tried to move him forward.

"Jump, Alex!" he heard Maude shout. "Jump into the next square!"

He thought he felt the owl's wing brush his shoulder as he jumped and watched dreamily as it flew far, far away into the distance where the trees of the big forest stood. "He may come back!" flashed through Alex's mind. "No the dragon won't let him," he thought. Then he landed, with a rather hard bump, on top of a small, bushy pine tree.

Purple mountains surrounded him, high and remote, some of them tipped with snow. The sky was clear and blue with wispy clouds, and the air was crisp. The area seemed quite unpopulated and hushed as if waiting for something to happen.

"Well, you finally made it," said Daisy's voice, "and if you think it's been lots of fun here, you're wrong."

She lay in the tree several branches below him looking up at him with her green eyes.

"I had to help all those small animals," explained Alex, "the

 mole and the rabbits and the little mice. They would have lost their lives."

"Dear me," breathed Daisy, narrowing her eyes, "the poor, wee mice and the mole. No wonder I wasn't invited." She jumped off her branch and stalked off, tail stiffly upright.

"Oh, Daisy," said Alex, somewhat apologetically, tumbling down off the tree, "you didn't miss anything. It wasn't a cat sort of thing, really."

Daisy sniffed and smoothed her whiskers, staring off into space as if she couldn't care less.

"I see. Well, the dragon," she yawned deliciously and scratched her ear in a thoughtful way, "has promised me something special. Something," she gave him a quick glance, "that you might call a *real* cat sort of thing. Want to come?"

"Oh, yes," said Alex, because what other answer could he give? He felt quite exhausted from his day's work and had been looking forward to a rest and perhaps a chat with the dragon.

"Where *is* the dragon?" he inquired.

"Up there," Daisy looked towards the top of the purple peak upon which they stood. They were near the very top on one of the rough pathways that seemed to criss-cross through the rocks, stunted pine trees, and brush.

As Alex followed her glance, he could see puffs of smoke rising into the air. The dragon was smoking, as usual. They climbed the mountain, and the dragon was soon within sight.

"Alex," he said, happily. "How good to see you!"

"You didn't know me at all before," grumbled Alex before he could stop himself.

"Hurt feelings?" queried the dragon. "Daisy and I discussed

that." He hesitated as he re-lit his pipe and inhaled deeply. "It was like a time-machine, dear Alex, you went back to a time before I had met you in that pile of leaves. *Now*, if I met you almost any time, all the way back to our last encounter in the Middle Ages, I would know you. And," he continued graciously, "I would always be very glad to see you."

"And I glad to see you," replied Alex in great relief, and he meant it—every word.

"Well, that's settled," announced Daisy. "Come on, dragon, it's magic time. Remember what you promised. Alex," she said sharply, "don't go to sleep."

The boy had put one arm around the dragon's waist and rested his head against his warm, scaly body, which was surprisingly soft.

Alex opened his eyes very wide to stay awake and, as he did, he noticed a great many stars of all sizes and colors above them in the sky. The sky was black now, and the stars seemed to come closer and closer with a slight, spinning motion. He heard a faint chime of bells at the same time.

"You've heard of the Dog Star, of course," Daisy whispered in his ear, rather sneeringly, "but you are about to see . . ." she took a sort of dance step and held up one paw towards a greenish star revolving slowly on its points, getting larger and larger until it came to a halt touching the very top of the mountain.

"... the Cat Star!"

Alex's eyes were dazzled by its strange green light and by a sparkling mist that seemed to drift across its surface.

"Come on," he heard Daisy shout as she made a running leap. "This is *my* dream."

"I'll be right there, if you need me," the dragon's voice said faintly as Alex, somewhat reluctantly, followed Daisy.

He landed in a patch of strange, glittering fog and could barely see Daisy's dim figure up ahead. But was it Daisy? The air cleared, and before him was an open gate that seemed to be the entrance to a park. The cat going through it was grey. Rushing forward, along one of several broad, dirt paths, he called Daisy's name.

He felt a warm, furry body rub against his leg. "Yes," came a meowing answer, "I'm Daisy."

He looked down but saw instantly that this was not Daisy but a large white Angora.

"You're not Daisy," said Alex crossly.

"No, *I* am," said a grey tabby.

A Siamese appeared from behind a clump of ferns. "Did someone call my name?" The blue, slightly-crossed eyes stared at him, hopefully.

Alex put his hands on his hips and glared at all of them, but it occurred to him that other cats might be called Daisy too. After all, he was not the only boy named Alex.

"Well, you're not *my* Daisy," he said, "she's white and black and orange."

"A calico," hissed the Siamese. "Well, it's a matter of taste, I suppose." With that, they all drifted away.

Before him was a sunny park filled with giant palms, hung with brown fruit. There were masses of flowering bushes and trees of every kind. Some branches had fallen and lay across small, rushing streams. Cats sat fishing by the sides of deep pools with bamboo poles. Their heads nodding sleepily under straw hats. Others were wading and making sudden grabs with their paws when fish splashed in the water. Beneath the bushes, dappled by leaves, were hundreds of cats. They were sleeping curled around each other, purring like a distant hum of bees. There were kittens of every color biting and nipping with their sharp baby teeth, rolling over and under each other as they played.

Alex watched, enchanted. They were all different and all beautiful. It would be hard to choose the nicest one. But where was Daisy? It was hard to keep his eyes on this kaleidoscope of cats that seemed to change every moment, but he was soon sure that Daisy was not there.

He took off on another path and soon saw a meadow of grass and flowers with masses of blue and yellow butterflies hovering over it. They were darting up and down in a strange way. As Alex got closer he could see raised cat's paws extending here and there from the tall grass. In sudden leaps, some would be silhouetted against the sky for an instant, or a tail would show as its owner sank out of sight.

He walked along the meadow's edge until he came to a hill, which he climbed. He had a wonderful view of impassioned cats chasing butterflies, but Daisy was nowhere to be found.

Sitting down to rest and think, he discovered some wild strawberries to eat. How nice it would be to stretch out here in the warm sun. His head nodded, and he came to with a start.

"No, I must find Daisy," he thought, "she's got to be here someplace."

He walked further, passing a sandy place where cats rolled, wriggling on their backs and waving wild paws in the air. Around its edge were others nibbling at grasses and herbs, which they sniffed in a lingering, suspicious way. It seemed to Alex as if every cat on earth had been carried to this star.

"And cats certainly like warm weather," he said, wiping his wet brow with one sleeve.

The question "what does Daisy like best?" came suddenly into his mind, and he saw pictures of shrimp, fish, and cream. "Maybe that's where she'll be. Where there's *food!*"

He gave a shout and a startled black kitten rolled down the hill. Running to the path below, he continued on his way.

He began to notice small signs with words scratched

on them. He read "Climbing Trees" and "Moon Song." Then one so tiny and worn that he almost missed it, "Find Mousie."

"Aha!" thought Alex with a rush of hope, and he followed that path back through some trees. Before he reached the place, he smelled it—a strong, unmistakable odor. He found himself in a semi-enclosed cement area that was full of enormous wedges of Swiss cheese dotted with holes.

"Like part of a big cellar," Alex thought. All through the cheese wedges and over them, cats crept slowly on their bellies, their eyes glowing feverishly.

A loud bell bonged suddenly, and Daisy's voice called loud and clear.

"*I* won!"

There she was, black, orange, and white, like a tiger, and in her mouth was—a *tin* mouse.

Alex let out his breath in relief. It was a game. After all, cats did love games.

"Daisy," he said, and his voice was full of love.

"Oh, Alex," she said, the tin mouse's tail flipping carelessly up and down in her pink mouth. "Isn't this a wonderful place?"

He nodded wordlessly.

Daisy ate a good deal of the cheese, which was real, and then found a fountain that spouted cream. Her stomach was so round and full that her legs looked like sticks stuck into a fur ball. She could barely crawl into his lap.

"Time to go," said Alex dreamily, almost asleep, and the ground turned slippery and green, seeming to tilt beneath them. They slid down its slope going faster and faster until they landed with a soft thud on the quilt that lay across Alex's bed.

"That was my dream," purred Daisy and soon they were both asleep.

The Sixth Night

lex and Aunt Rachel spent the next day, their last day together, doing the things they liked best. They walked down to the beach and had a lunchtime picnic—sandwiches and a thermos of hot cocoa. The wind was off the water and stung their faces when it blew too hard. Gulls wheeled in the sky showing a grey side or a white side as they turned. Protected by one of the big rocks, Aunt Rachel and Alex built a fire with driftwood and toasted marshmallows.

Aunt Rachel's face was rosy from the wind. She looked at Alex, who had stopped eating and was staring out to sea, and at his finger, which was tracing the round face of a cat with whiskers in the sand.

"Bet I know what you're thinking about."

Alex jumped. He had been thinking about a good number of things, an octopus and King Neptune among them.

"Daisy?" he asked, for he knew what she meant.

"She's a darling."

"Yes," replied Alex rather miserably. "I wish I could take her with me."

"She'd never like the city, Alex. No places to explore, just the inside of an apartment. She's a real outdoor cat and comes and goes as she likes, though she spends most of the winter in front of my fire."

"I'll really miss her," said Alex sadly, "and you, too," he added in a kind way.

"Well, who's saying goodbye?" his aunt said cheerfully, giving him a quick hug. "You can visit anytime, holidays, next week. . . . you could even come and spend all summer with Daisy!"

Alex felt his spirits lift as if carried wildly upward by the next gust of wind.

They struggled back up the hill carrying the picnic basket, their eyes tearing and their noses running.

"How about a movie tonight?" his aunt panted.

She stopped by the apple tree before going in the house. "All the rest of my apples are on the ground," she observed. "I guess I'll have to make some more pies before you leave. Some for you and some for me."

That evening they saw a Western in a weather-beaten old theater smelling of years of buttered popcorn.

Alex said goodnight to his aunt when they got home and suddenly felt so sleepy that he could hardly walk upstairs. He left his clothes in a sandy pile on the floor and was about to climb into bed when he saw something shining on one of the quilt's patches. He saw with delight that it was a whisker. Daisy had left it for him to remember her by, he felt sure, and cat's whiskers meant good luck.

He knew he would see her soon on his next visit. Her whisker was a reminder not to forget her. "As if I could," he thought tenderly.

He picked it up carefully and wrapped it in a paper napkin left in his pocket from the picnic. It wouldn't get lost like the little lace handkerchief.

As he crawled under the quilt, he looked at the patch where he had found the whisker. Embroidered flowers stuck here and there in a yellow background and an odd-looking gnome with a watering can was standing in one corner.

"Who's he?" thought Alex without much interest, and shut his eyes.

Hot sun was filling the attic room with light. No air seemed to be coming through the open window. Alex woke up on his bed thinking about going swimming and cold lemonade. He saw with some surprise that he was wearing khaki shorts. It was certainly much too warm for quilts. Leaning out the window he noticed in confusion that the apple tree was covered with small green apples. It's summer, he thought, but last summer or next summer? On the tree branch just below him lay an old boy-scout knife. Caught between the limb and the tree, it must have lain there for years. But when he climbed out the window and picked it up, he noticed it was not rusted but clean and bright as if it had been used yesterday. He put it in his pocket; it fit comfortably as if it belonged there. He slid the rest of the way down the tree and landed in a cloud of dust.

The dirt had turned to brown powder and the green grass to yellow stubble. As he crossed the yard, he saw Daisy asleep on her side in the shadow of the tool shed. A bird flapped its wings in the dust not three feet away from her, its beak wide open as it gasped for air. She was too hot to notice.

"Whew! It's a scorcher," said Alex to himself. He remembered hearing others say this in July or August.

The bird flew away, and Daisy barely opened one eye. But she opened *both* as a strange, small figure passed them and went through a garden gate that Alex had never seen before. It was a gnome carrying a watering can, the very sort of gnome sold in some stores to decorate yards. Those were made of plaster but this one, although it seemed to have a chip in its painted shoe, certainly seemed alive. When she saw what it was, Daisy shut her eyes in complete boredom, but Alex followed him into what seemed to be a fenced garden.

The remains of dried-up flowers filled the beds. A drooping daisy lay moaning faintly, and a rose hung listlessly against its stake. A geranium with a few bright-red petals had its feet stuck into a dry pot. There were a few jagged dandelions to add a little color, but what a dreary place this was!

The gnome was stomping stiffly around trying to water them all with an empty watering can. Alex saw several of the gnome's brothers. One, in a blue apron, was seemingly trying to dig some dead weeds out with a broken shovel and another was uselessly raking the hard ground.

"What are you all doing?" Alex heard himself ask.

They turned awkwardly and stared at him with their surprised, painted eyes.

"We're gardening, of course," they all said at once in creaky, old voices.

"You call this gardening?" questioned Alex in a rather bossy way. "What you need is water, lots and lots of water." He kicked at the ground and watched the dust rise like smoke. "Everything will be dead soon at this rate," he said. "Why don't you get the hose out for goodness' sake?"

"Not allowed," said the watering-can gnome. "Rationed."

"There's been no rain in months," said the raking gnome rather desperately. "We're doing the best we can."

"Not a cloud in the sky," reflected the gnome with the broken shovel, looking up and wiping his brow gloomily.

"He's not sweating," thought Alex, annoyed, "he's only made of plaster." But he looked up at the sky, too.

"Look," he said suddenly, pointing at the far blue horizon, "over there, aren't those . . .?"

"Clouds," shouted the gnomes. A slight animation crossed their faces. "*Rain* clouds?"

They all stared at them thoughtfully as the clouds blew quickly closer.

"*Rain* clouds!" they then proclaimed in delight.

"Oh, I do hope it rains here so I can fill my watering can," said the first gnome.

The others joined arms at the elbows and did a clumsy, jogging dance.

Alex watched as the clouds piled into one large, flat, grey area, that seemed to be caught on the top branches of the apple tree. The sun was hidden, which made it slightly cooler, but nothing happened. The cloud just hung there motionless and dark. Alex looked at it curiously, waiting. What a strange cloud! It reminded him of the ones in comic strips that hung over someone's head when they were sad.

The gnomes waited too, standing under it hopefully. Daisy rolled onto her back and curled up her front paws but didn't wake up. Nothing happened.

"Well," said Alex loudly in all this hushed waiting. "I guess I'd better go see what's going on."

He climbed quickly up the apple tree and looked over the edge of the cloud. Far off, on its furthest side was a sort of bumpy, grey castle. In front of it sat the dragon glowing colorfully in the sun, which still shone brightly there. Alex immediately pulled himself up and climbed onto the dark surface. He bobbed and shook on his way to reach the dragon.

"Dragon," he called, "it's me, Alex!"

Soon they were face to face, and the dragon lay down his pipe. "I've been making rain clouds, Alex," he said pleasantly, "and just thought I'd bring one over this way."

"Oh, dragon," said Alex admiringly, "you always know what's needed, but why isn't it raining?"

"Not raining?" answered the dragon in surprise. "Dear me, I haven't the foggiest idea. There's water inside, of course, I filled them up myself at the mountain stream."

Alex knelt down and placed his ear on the cloudy surface. He could hear a sloshing, bubbling sound inside. Exactly the sort of noise you might hear in a balloon when making a water bomb. He sat on his heels and thought while the dragon watched him hopefully.

"Ah," Alex said abruptly, as if a bell had rung. He took out the boy-scout knife and plunged it deep into the cloud.

There was a happy shout from the gnomes below, and he rushed about punching holes as fast as he could and jumping violently up and down to squeeze the water out. In no time it was raining hard. He could almost see the grass turning green, and the flowers lifting their heads when he peered

over the cloud's edge. Daisy had disappeared.

"Good going, Alex!" chortled the dragon's happy voice. "What a good idea!"

Alex stood on tiptoe and kissed the dragon's cheek. "I'll miss you," he said.

The dragon gave a noisy sort of gulp and turned red-violet. His eyes filled with water that spilled down his nose. He held up a limp paw.

"Oh, dear, I believe it's raining," he gasped.

"It's raining down below," said Alex gently, "not here."

The dragon shut his eyes and lowered his head.

"It's just . . ." he coughed.

"I know," said Alex.

They sat together in silence for a few minutes.

"By the way," asked Alex curiously, "what is your real name? It can't be 'dragon.' It would be like calling me 'boy' or Daisy 'cat.'"

The dragon lit his pipe again. It always seemed to be going out. After a few puffs, he returned to his normal color.

"Well," he said, "it's rather an unusual one. I'm called 'Imagination.' But you could call me Magio. *Joe* Magio," he laughed merrily at his own joke.

Alex thought it a rather poor one but remembered that the dragon was hundreds of years old.

"What am I going to do without you?" Alex asked miserably.

"Without me?" the dragon replied, aghast. "*Without* me? Oh, my dear boy, never! I'll be around, you'll see. Not in the flesh, perhaps," he gazed down at his curving stomach and clawed toes and flicked his tail once or twice as if to make sure it was still there. "But always in the old noggin'," he tapped Alex firmly on the head.

"Ouch," said Alex.

"See," said the dragon eagerly, "It will be just like that. You'll know I'm there suddenly. You may even say 'hello, dragon.' In fact," said the dragon, hugging Alex, "it must always be '*hello* dragon' and never 'goodbye.'"

"Yes," said Alex. He didn't exactly understand but, somehow, he felt better anyway.

"Tomorrow, I'm going home," he said.

"Ah," said the dragon, "well, I must be off today. This very moment in fact." And, as he spoke, he arose and took several steps backwards and up onto the higher part of the cloud where the castle stood. This area, to Alex's alarm, seemed to be separating from the rest. Puffs rose from the dragon's pipe and made little clouds above him in the sky.

Alex stared in dismay as the dragon disappeared rapidly on his own cloud. He grew smaller and smaller, but Alex could see him waving.

"Hello, Alex!" he heard the dragon shout from afar.

"Hello, dragon!" shouted Alex over and over until he had completely disappeared.

Lying down on the cloud, Alex thrust his hand deep inside it and, catching some water in his palm, cooled his face. He settled comfortably onto its fluffy surface and was not at all surprised, sometime later, to find himself on the quilt in his room. Rubbing his eyes, he looked up to see Aunt Rachel smiling down at him.

"All packed and ready to go?" she said. "Yes," he answered sleepily.

"Well, I'll go down and make breakfast."

As she left, he saw that his clothes were neatly hung over the chair. Hurriedly checking to see if Daisy's whisker was still there, he was relieved to find it. It hadn't disappeared like the little lace handkerchief. He folded up the dream quilt and put it away in his great-great-grandfather's chest.

"Until the next time," he said to no one in particular. Although no one seemed to be there, he was thinking of the dragon and Maude, and especially of Daisy.

It was time to go home and Alex found himself not sad but happy. "Because," he told himself, "as the dragon would say, 'there are adventures everywhere and anytime.'" And he rushed down the stairs to meet them.

Acknowledgments

The author and artist wish to thank the team at Charles E. Tuttle Co. for believing in our dream and making it come true: Peter Ackroyd, Roberta Scimone, Kathryn Sky-Peck, Fran Skelly, Julie McManus, Isabelle Bleecker, Michael L. Kerber, and Lorrie Andonian.

We would also like to thank Monte Farber, Mary Jane Seely Gary Bartolini, Toni Lind, Kit-Kat, Vivian at VJS Frames, Michael and Diane at Montauk Printers, Ed and Jeff at Cameron Photo, Mary at the East Hampton Business Service, and our friends at The Golden Eagle.

We also wish to acknowledge the many great children's book authors and artists who have always given us much joy and inspiration.